Just One Of The Family

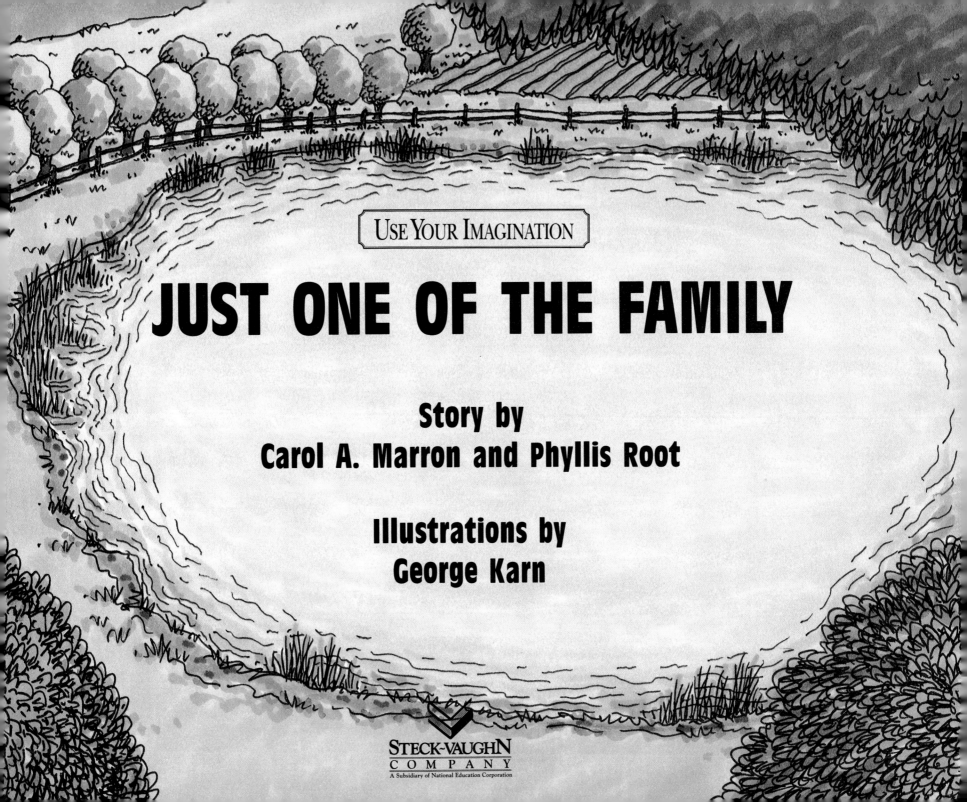

USE YOUR IMAGINATION

JUST ONE OF THE FAMILY

Story by
Carol A. Marron and Phyllis Root

Illustrations by
George Karn

STECK-VAUGHN
COMPANY
A Subsidiary of National Education Corporation

FOR VIVIAN
AND GALE
—C.M.

FOR THE
CHILDRENS
WRITER'S
GUILD
—P.R.

KATHY
—G.K.

First Steck-Vaughn Edition 1993
Published by Steck-Vaughn Company

Art Direction: Su Lund

1 2 3 4 5 6 7 8 9 W 97 96 95 94 93 92

ISBN 0-8114-8404-1

After the last potato was dug and the last apple picked, Ed said to Nellie, "We've worked like bears. I'm going to curl up and sleep all winter."

"Nonsense," said Nellie. "Let's take a vacation."

"We can't leave the cow," said Ed. "Or the goat, or the lambs, or the hen."

"We'll take them along,"
said Nellie. "They're all
part of the family."

7

Nellie found everything she needed in the attic.

"Some gloves for Aunt Bessie and a derby for Grandpa. Sweaters for the twins and a blanket for Baby Rhodie."

9

"It'll never work," warned Ed as they drove away. "We look worse than a rooster in a rainstorm."

"Don't be silly," said Nellie, straightening her hat. "We make a lovely family."

"I'm as hungry as a horse," said Ed when they stopped for lunch.

Grandpa was hungry, too.

"Do you always let him eat the flowers?" asked the waitress.

"Only if they're absolutely fresh," replied Nellie.

After lunch they stopped at a museum.

Aunt Bessie liked the Victorian hat display . . .

. . . and Grandpa found
the flag exhibit tasteful.

Ed wanted to see the model farm.

But the museum guard asked them all to leave when he caught the twins leaping back and forth over the mummy case.

That night they stayed in a motel.

"You call this a vacation?" complained Ed as they got ready for bed. "I've had more fun pitching hay with a dinner fork."

"It's a marvelous vacation,"
said Nellie, tucking in the twins.
"Tomorrow will be even better."

But the next day they didn't get very far. Aunt Bessie insisted on stopping at every scenic overlook.

That night they had to camp in the forest.

Ed built a fire and Nellie passed around the marshmallows.

"I've had better times pulling pigs from a mud puddle," grumbled Ed.

But he helped the twins button their pajamas and told them a bedtime story.

The next morning Grandpa wanted to go mountain climbing.

"What a fine, strong family you have," a passing ranger remarked. "You all seem to enjoy the out-of-doors."

"You might say we were born in a barnyard," Ed agreed.

25

At the seashore they took a ride on an excursion boat. Aunt Bessie fell in love with the foghorn.

"Is your aunt all right?" the captain inquired.

"Crazy as a lovesick calf," Ed told him. "But what can we do? She's one of the family."

Before they left they had their picture taken. Tired but happy, they headed for home.

"Nonsense," said Nellie. "Wait till you see where we're taking the family next year."

31

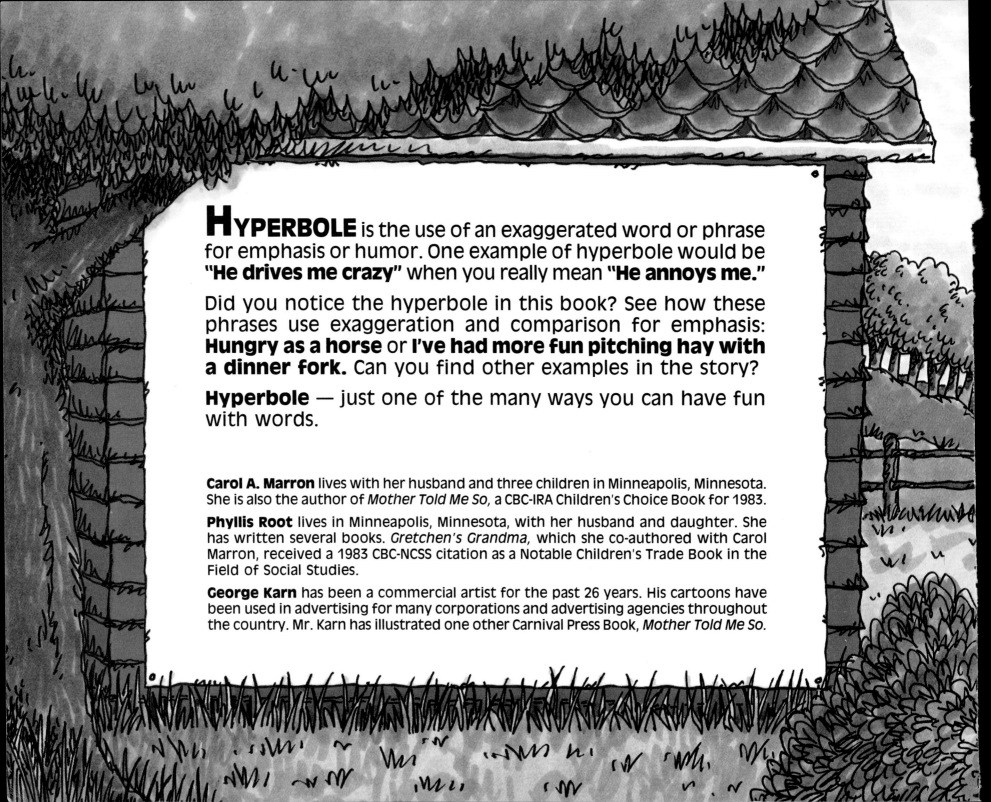

HYPERBOLE is the use of an exaggerated word or phrase for emphasis or humor. One example of hyperbole would be **"He drives me crazy"** when you really mean **"He annoys me."**

Did you notice the hyperbole in this book? See how these phrases use exaggeration and comparison for emphasis: **Hungry as a horse** or **I've had more fun pitching hay with a dinner fork.** Can you find other examples in the story?

Hyperbole — just one of the many ways you can have fun with words.

Carol A. Marron lives with her husband and three children in Minneapolis, Minnesota. She is also the author of *Mother Told Me So,* a CBC-IRA Children's Choice Book for 1983.

Phyllis Root lives in Minneapolis, Minnesota, with her husband and daughter. She has written several books. *Gretchen's Grandma,* which she co-authored with Carol Marron, received a 1983 CBC-NCSS citation as a Notable Children's Trade Book in the Field of Social Studies.

George Karn has been a commercial artist for the past 26 years. His cartoons have been used in advertising for many corporations and advertising agencies throughout the country. Mr. Karn has illustrated one other Carnival Press Book, *Mother Told Me So.*